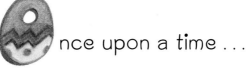nce upon a time . . .
there were **3** bears named "Brown"
who lived in the town of

LEO was the papa, **IRMA** was the mama, and **PATRICK** was the little boy.

Visit www.hyperionchildrensbooks.com

Printed in Singapore

First Edition

1 3 5 7 9 10 8 6 4 2

This book was set in Tweed Medium.

Library of Congress Cataloging-in-Publication Data
Hayes, Geoffrey.
Patrick and the big bully / story and pictures by Geoffrey Hayes.—1st ed.
p.   cm.
Summary: When Patrick Bear meets a bully on the way to the store, pretending to be
a dragon helps him deals with the situation.
ISBN 0-7868-0717-2 (hardcover)
[1. Bullies—Fiction. 2. Bears—Fiction.] I. Title.
PZ7.H31455 Bh 2001
[E]—dc21
00-63378

TED

LITTLE SUNSHINE & WEAVER

THE ADVENTURES OF PATRICK BROWN

PATRICK and the BIG BULLY
by Geoffrey Hayes

HYPERION BOOKS FOR CHILDREN
NEW YORK

HELGA

OLLIE

EXTENSION

Patrick was busy being a dragon when Mama Bear came to the door. "Patrick," she said, "would you please go to OLLIE'S store and buy us some cookies for lunch?"

ROAR!

"Way down there?"
said Patrick.

"It's just around the
corner," Mama explained.
She gave him some money.
"Here, get one **DOLLAR'S** worth."

"But what if I run into some **BIG KIDS?**" asked Patrick.

"Oh, I wouldn't worry about that. You're a **DRAGON** ... remember? Let's hear that dragon roar."

ROAR!

Patrick walked down
the block, practicing his roar.

"Hey, **STRIPEY-PANTS!** Is that the dollar you owe me?" he growled.

"I don't owe you a dollar.
Please move, Big Bear.
I'm going to buy **COOKIES**
for Mama."

"Are **NOT!**"
growled Big Bear.

"Am **SO!**" cried Patrick.

Patrick raced off down the block.

Big Bear ran right after him.

HEY!
Out of
my way!

Patrick ran into **Helga's** garden.

EXTENSION

Big Bear was
right behind him.

Patrick squeezed through
a **HOLE** in the fence. . . .

Patrick saw Ollie's store across the street. He hurried inside.

The little bell over the door went DING!
And **OLLIE ARWOOD**
came in from the kitchen.
"Hello, Patrick," he called. "What can
I do for you today?"

"Mama sent me
to buy **COOKIES**,"
said Patrick.

"Well, we have a big selection. What kind?"

Patrick looked at all the different cookies under the counter.

"May I use your phone?" he asked.

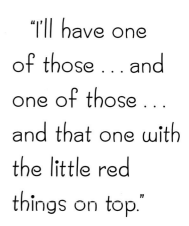

"Hello, Mama? It's me. What kind of cookies? Oh . . . okay!

"She said to get my favorite.

"I'll have one of those . . . and one of those . . . and that one with the little red things on top."

Ollie threw an extra cookie in the bag.

"It's on the house," he said.

Patrick handed Ollie the money. Then, he peeped out the window.

"Big Bear is chasing me," he explained.

Oh, he is, is he?

Ollie let Patrick out the back door.

"Say hello to your mom for me," he called.

"I will," said Patrick.

He didn't see Big Bear until it was too late!

"There you are, STRIPEY-PANTS. You owe me that bag of COOKIES!"

"Do NOT!" cried Patrick. He took off across the vacant lot as fast as his legs would carry him.

It was his good friend, **TED**.

TED'S FORT

BINOCULARS

MAP

DIARY

BLANKET

SNACKS

COMPASS

Ted lowered a rope ladder, and Patrick
climbed up to Ted's fort in the tree branches.

When Big Bear tried to climb up, Ted dumped a bunch of leaves and twigs on top of him ... while Patrick slid down the other side of the tree.

He was back in
HELGA'S GARDEN!

!

BUTTERFLIES

UH-OH!
TOO LATE!

SUNDIAL

LAUNDRY

Patrick hid inside a flowerpot.

Big Bear found a
COOKIE. It had fallen out
of Patrick's bag.

"**OOOW!** One with little red things on top!
Thanks, wimp!"
He popped the cookie in his mouth.
"Who's there?" said Helga.

Helga saw Big Bear all covered with leaves and mud. "EEK!" she shrieked. "There's a **DRAGON** in my snapdragons!"

When Patrick heard the word "dragon," he thought of Mama Bear saying "You're a dragon . . . remember?"

And that made him want to . . .

Patrick went right up to Big Bear
and said, "Listen, I don't owe YOU
anything! You owe ME a cookie!"

Then, he marched out of the garden.

He ran into **PAPA BEAR**, who was on his way home for lunch.

"Hey, Sport!"

"Hi, Papa! Want to hear my dragon roar?"

"So, did you meet any BIG KIDS out there?"

"NO," said Patrick. "Just a big MUDDY-PANTS!"

He told Mama and Papa the whole story. Then, they all had cookies— and Patrick's dragon had a NAP!